NORTH SEA

BERWICK-UPON-TWE

Salmon

CARLISLE

Hermitage Castle

Scott

Ferry Crossings

ST ANDREWS

Balmoral

Golf

PERTH

Mary, Queen of Scots

Edinburgh Castle

GLASGOW

Loch Tay

Highland Cattle

Loch Lomond

Robert Burns

Ben Nevis

Loch Awe

PRESTWICK

AYR

Dunure Castle

OBAN

Fishing

BUTE

ARRAN

MULL

JURA

IONA

COLONSAY

ISLAY

TIREE

ATLANTIC OCEAN

D0429088

From the Borders to John o'Groats, Scotland is a land of surprises — snow-capped mountains and deep, still lochs; busy little fishing villages and vigorous industrial towns; fairytale castles and sturdy cottages. Its people are wanderers — they can be found in every corner of the world; but they all remember their roots, and take pride in their Scottish heritage.

History, beauty and romance — here is a fleeting glimpse of that small country the whole world has heard of.

Cover: *Kilchurn Castle and Loch Awe, Argyll*

Title page: *Urquhart Castle and Loch Ness*

Acknowledgments
Photographs supplied by: Ian Anderson: title page and pages 28, 34 (bottom), 35 (top and bottom), 50 (top) and 51 (top and bottom); Britain on View: pages 8 (top), 17 (bottom), 24 (top and bottom); Conoco (UK) Ltd: page 30; Elspeth Crichton: back cover and pages 7, 9 (top and bottom), 10, 10-11, 12, 36 (top), 38 (bottom), 38-9; M E Daly: page 6; Robert Harding Picture Library: pages 18 (top), 20 (top), 25, 26 (bottom), 48-9 (top); David Henrie: pages 20 (bottom), 21, 44 (top and bottom); Hurlston Design Ltd: front endpaper; Livingston Development Corporation: page 14; Rob Norman: pages 16-17, 18 (bottom), 19 (top, middle and bottom), 36-7, 41 (top and bottom); Paul Popper Ltd: page 34; J Roy: 50 (bottom); Royal Botanic Garden, Edinburgh: page 13 (top and bottom); Scottish Tourist Board: pages 5, 8 (bottom), 22 (top and bottom), 23, 26 (top), 27 (top and bottom), 29 (top and bottom), 31 (top and bottom), 32 (top and bottom), 33 (top and bottom), 38 (top), 40 (top and bottom), 42, 43 (top and bottom), 45 (top and bottom), 46, 47 (top and bottom), 48-9 (bottom), 49; Tony Stone (Worldwide) Ltd: cover and pages 4-5, 15.

Designed by Graham Marlow.

British Library Cataloguing in Publication Data
Melvin, Eric
    Scotland.—(Discovering)
    1. Scotland—Juvenile literature
    I. Title   II. Series
    941.1085'8   DA757.5
    ISBN 0-7214-0946-6

Santa Rosa, Sept. 2, 1990. For Sam Morgan, youngest of the three fine kilted Clan Leask members to whom we look for the future in hope. Remember our Clan Motto "Virtute Cresco"! From his Chief, A. Leask of Leask

First edition

Published by Ladybird Books Ltd Loughborough Leicestershire UK
Ladybird Books Inc Lewiston Maine 04240 USA

DISCOVERING
Scotland

written by
ERIC MELVIN

Ladybird Books

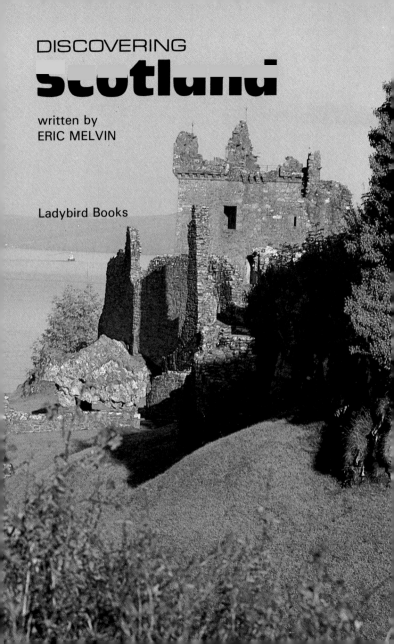

Glen Lyon, Perthshire

Drawn by thoughts of mist-covered mountains and heather-clad glens, about eight million people visit Scotland each year. Many of them return time after time, finding something new on each visit.

Some prefer the remote, unspoilt Highlands, parts of which date back 750 million years. The Gaelic culture and language still flourish there, and farming and fishing are both important.

Others prefer the Lowlands and the capital city of Edinburgh, famous for its yearly Festival of Music and

Drama. Two-thirds of Scotland's population of five million live in the Lowlands, where the traditional industries of coal, steel and shipbuilding have been joined by micro electronics and oil.

Although it is part of the United Kingdom, Scotland still has its own laws, its own Church, and its own educational system. There are Scottish banks as well, which have their own colourful banknotes with portraits of famous Scots like David Livingstone.

Pipers at Traquair House, in the Borders

5

Jedburgh Abbey

Visitors coming from the south must pass through
Border country, famous for sheep farming. The first
sheep there were brought by Cistercian monks in the
eleventh century. Melrose, Dryburgh, Kelso, and
Jedburgh all have magnificent abbeys built by the
monks. Near Dumfries is the charming Sweetheart

Abbey, built for Lady Devorgilla in memory of her husband John Balliol. (She also founded Balliol College, Oxford.)

Sadly, these abbeys were destroyed when the English invaded Scotland in 1544, and were never fully restored.

Abbotsford

Readers of *Rob Roy* and other novels and poems by Sir Walter Scott would find a visit to Abbotsford very rewarding. The house, which stands beside the River Tweed, was the writer's home until his death in 1832. It has been kept much as he knew it, filled with the historical relics that he collected.

Borderers are noted for their sturdy independence. In the lawless days of the sixteenth century, many Border families had their own private armies – fighting their neighbours as well as the English! This independence is

Riding the Marches

seen in the annual Common Riding of the Marches, when each Border town parades round its boundaries.

There is also intense rivalry amongst the rugby football teams of the Border towns – a rivalry which produces some great players. On one occasion, no fewer than eleven of the players picked to play for Scotland were from Border clubs!

South-west of Edinburgh lie the Pentland Hills. They helped in defence in Roman times, and in the seventeenth century these same hills sheltered Covenanters fleeing from religious persecution.

The writer Robert Louis Stevenson lived for a while in nearby Swanston village.

Today the Pentlands are enjoyed by walkers, fishermen and – perhaps surprisingly – skiers. Hillend is Britain's largest artificial ski slope (shown above and below).

Watched over by its famous castle, Edinburgh stretches out towards the surrounding hills, with a skyline known the world over.

Down from the castle runs the street called the Royal Mile, centre of Edinburgh's historic Old Town. Some of the buildings there are well worth a visit: Gladstone's Land (17th century), John Knox's House (16th century) and Huntly House (also 16th century) are amongst them.

Right at the foot of the Royal Mile is the palace of Holyroodhouse. Here you will be shown the tiny room where David Rizzio was stabbed to death in front of Mary, Queen of Scots.

Arthur's Seat

Edinburgh Castle

10

Holyroodhouse is the Queen's official residence.
Following a tradition set by Queen Victoria, a piper
plays early each morning to wake the Queen.

The palace stands in the shadow of Arthur's Seat, the
remains of a volcano 325 million years old. Not far
away is Meadowbank Stadium, from time to time home
of the Commonwealth Games.

Every year, for three weeks, Edinburgh plays host to
performers and visitors from all over the world, during
the International Festival of Music and Drama. One of
the most spectacular events is a floodlit Military Tattoo,
held on the Castle Esplanade.

Edinburgh's main street is Princes Street, lying straight as a ruler from east to west across the city. On one side are the attractive Princes Street Gardens, and across from there is the New Town, planned in the eighteenth century.

The best view is from the top of the Scott Monument – but you will have to climb two hundred and eighty-seven steps to see it!

At the east end is St Andrew's Square. Several life assurance companies have their headquarters there, and it is said to be the richest square in Europe.

At the other end is Charlotte Square. It was designed by Robert Adam in 1791 and is a superb example of Georgian architecture. Number 7 has been restored to its former grandeur by the National Trust for Scotland.

Charlotte Square

Royal Botanic Garden

There are many parks and other open spaces to enjoy in Edinburgh. One great favourite is the Botanic Garden – only ten minutes by bus from Princes Street. Here you can see some of the world's most beautiful and exotic plants including a palm tree that is nearly two hundred years old. The collection of rhododendrons is the largest in Britain.

Another favourite is Edinburgh Zoo, whose inhabitants include several of the world's most endangered species. There's an afternoon Penguin Parade, and a Children's Farm – both very popular.

Just west of Edinburgh is Livingston. It is one of Scotland's five New Towns, and one of the most vigorous industrial and commercial centres in Scotland. Many electronics firms are based in the town, which is said to be part of Scotland's "Silicon Glen". (Two-thirds of Britain's micro chips are made in Scotland.)

Livingston

There are only two landmarks to break the rich, low-lying farmland of East Lothian. One is Berwick Law, another extinct volcano, and the massive Traprain Law, an important Iron Age hill fort.

On the coast, Tantallon Castle broods, destroyed by Cromwell's soldiers in 1651. Not far away, in the Firth of Forth, is the strangely-shaped Bass Rock. Once a prison, it is now a bird sanctuary.

Near Dunbar, further along the coast, is Torness, one of Scotland's nuclear power stations.

Tantallon Castle ▶

In 1964 the Queen opened the Forth Road Bridge. This suspension bridge (600 m long) replaced a ferry started by Queen Margaret in the eleventh century. Next to it stands the Forth Railway Bridge (840 m long), which was completed in 1890. It was considered one of the great feats of engineering of its time, though fifty-seven men were killed building it. The bridge still carries the mainline rail traffic to the north and east of Scotland.

On the other side of the Forth is the Kingdom of Fife, a title held proudly for hundreds of years. Indeed, Fife was the only one of the old Scottish counties that retained its status as a Region when Scottish local government was reorganised in 1975. Seaside holiday resorts, rolling farmland and quaint villages are all typical of Fife. Best known is Culross. It dates back to the sixteenth and seventeenth centuries, and is under the care of the National Trust for Scotland.

Bridging the Firth of Forth

Culross, Fife

Falkland Palace was once a popular hunting lodge of the Stuart kings. Work on the Renaissance-style palace was started by James IV in 1501. The royal Tennis Court there is the oldest in Scotland. It was built in 1539 and is still played on.

Further round the coast lies the East Neuk of Fife with its fishing villages of St Monans, Anstruther, Pittenweem and Crail. The old stone cottages with their red pantile roofs clustering round the little harbours make this part of Fife popular with artists.

Falkland Palace

In 1547 James III ordered that "the futball and the gowf be utterly cryit doon and nocht usit" because archery practice was being neglected. Both games of course continued to be played and St Andrews, with its Royal and Ancient Golf Club, is recognised world-wide as the

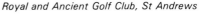

Royal and Ancient Golf Club, St Andrews

18

St Andrews Cathedral

home of golf. Indeed, a complete replica has been built in Japan! The University (1412) is the oldest in Scotland. In August each year, the main streets of the town are taken over for the Lammas Fair, a market dating back hundreds of years.

St Salvator's College, St Andrews

St Mary's College, St Andrews

Scone Palace, Perth

On the banks of the River Tay stands Perth, often called the Fair City. The old water works (1832) is now an imaginative Tourist Information Centre. Three kilometres north of Perth is the ancient palace of Scone, with Moot Hill close by. Here, traditionally, Scottish kings were crowned on the Stone of Destiny. The Stone was taken by Edward I in 1296 to place beneath the seat of the Coronation Chair at Westminster. Many Scots think the real Stone is still in Scotland!

Further north – about sixteen kilometres, on the road to Blairgowrie – is the world's tallest beech hedge. Planted in 1746, the hedge is 550m long and 35 m high.

Old Stirling Bridge

Stirling Castle

Perched on its massive rock, Stirling Castle dominates both the surrounding countryside and much of Scotland's turbulent history. During the long struggle for independence, the castle changed hands several times before being surrendered finally to Robert the Bruce after the battle of Bannockburn in 1314. During that battle, fought on the low-lying land beneath Stirling Castle, the Scottish army of eight thousand men destroyed the much larger English army of Edward II. The long war of independence had been won by Bruce, though fighting was to continue for many years. There is a statue of Bruce on the battlefield which was unveiled by the Queen in June 1964, and an Interpretation Centre tells of all that happened at the battle.

Festival Theatre

Pitlochry stands at "the gateway to the Highlands". The new Festival Theatre, opened by Prince Charles in 1981, started life in a large tent. The hydro-electric station is powered by the fast-flowing waters of the River Tummel. Salmon can be seen through the windows of a special fish ladder which helps them to climb upriver at spawning time.

A whisky distillery

Outside Pitlochry is one of Scotland's smallest whisky distilleries, Edradour. (Whisky means "water of life" in Gaelic.) There are over a hundred distilleries in Scotland. Whisky is made from fermented, malted barley smoked over a peat fire and mixed with pure water, and over five hundred different varieties are made.

Each year thousands of tourists come to find "their" tartan. The earliest known tartan (or "coloured cloth") dates from the third century, though most present-day tartans were created in the last century to satisfy the Victorian fashion for things Scottish. The Scottish Tartan Society's Museum in Comrie houses the world's largest collection.

The Tartan Museum, Comrie

Tartans and Highland clans are closely linked. (Clan simply means "children" in Gaelic, and "Mac" in a surname means "son of".) A clan is a large family all claiming kinship with their leader, the chief, and these families can trace their descent from the sixth century Scottish settlers who came from Ireland. Until the 1745 Jacobite Rebellion, the chiefs were all-powerful. After Bonnie Prince Charlie's failure to regain the throne for the Stuarts, however, the chiefs lost most of their authority.

On 16th April, 1746, the last Jacobite Rebellion was crushed on bleak Culloden Moor. Bonnie Prince Charlie's weakened army of four thousand exhausted

clansmen was routed by a much larger government force led by the Duke of Cumberland – Charlie's cousin. His orders to kill wounded Jacobites earned him the nickname "Butcher" Cumberland. A Visitors' Centre on the battlefield describes the Rebellion. Leanach Cottage, which survived the battle, is still to be seen, and also the mass burial graves of the clans.

A clan grave

24

Some of Scotland's most beautiful castles are to be found in Deeside. Craigievar, completed in 1626, might have come straight from a fairytale! Nearby Crathes (1553) has an ornamental garden and a yew hedge planted in 1702. Inside are fascinating painted ceilings completed in 1599. These castles were not just decorative, however. They offered protection against the raids of marauding clansmen sweeping down from the mountains to the west.

Craigievar Castle

Balmoral, on the River Dee

Balmoral has been the Royal Family's holiday home for nearly a hundred and fifty years. In 1852 Queen Victoria and Prince Albert bought the Balmoral estate beside the River Dee, and Prince Albert planned the present castle (which replaced the original mansion house) in north-east Scotland. To Queen Victoria, Balmoral was "dear Paradise", and to this day the castle remains a private retreat for the Royal Family: it is never open to the public. The grounds however can be visited when none of the Royal Family is in residence.

Highland Games are a popular summer event in many Scottish towns and villages. Athletic events such as tossing the caber take place against a background of music from piping and Highland Dancing competitions.

Throwing the hammer, at Bute Highland Games

According to tradition, Highland Games were first held at Braemar in Royal Deeside in the eleventh century. The present Braemar Highland Gathering was revived by Queen Victoria and is attended each year by the Royal Family when on holiday at nearby Balmoral.

The Royal Family at Braemar

Sportsmen from all over the world come to shoot game in Scotland, and large moorland estates are reserved for this expensive pastime. Each year 12th August signals the start of the grouse shooting season, and there is always a race to get the first grouse to the tables of London restaurants.

Since 1919, the Forestry Commission has managed thousands of hectares of woodland. New plantations cover the once-bare hillsides, providing much-needed jobs. Five Forest Parks, with Information Centres, camping and picnic sites, cater for visitors.

A forestry plantation

The spectacular Cairngorms include some of the country's highest mountains and offer a wide range of outdoor activities. Best known of these is probably skiing, and Aviemore has grown into Britain's major winter sports resort where, each season, thousands of skiers enjoy the slopes. At the top of the chairlift at 1067 m is the highest restaurant in Britain – the Ptarmigan Restaurant. Just north of Aviemore is the Loch Garten Nature Reserve. Here, in 1959, a pair of ospreys returned to breed and these rare birds can be seen from a special observation hut.

Aviemore

Skiing in the Cairngorms

In November 1970, an exploratory oil rig struck oil 176 kilometres east of Aberdeen. This discovery has transformed the quiet medieval university city into Europe's oil capital. The harbour with its busy fish market has seen a £15 million development to service the supply ships for the North Sea rigs, and many new jobs have been created as a result.

King's College, Aberdeen

In contrast, the "Granite City" still has some fine architecture from the past. Its university dates from the fifteenth century, the cathedral of St Machar from the twelfth century, and Provost Skene's House from the sixteenth century.

More recent fame is associated with the football team, as winners of the Scottish Cup, the Scottish League and the European Cup Winners' Cup.

Kirkwall Cathedral, Orkney

The most northerly place on the British mainland is John o'Groats, and the first of the seventy islands of the Orkneys lies just twelve kilometres north of there.

On Mainland Island, you can see Skara Brae, a complete Stone Age village, thousands of years old. Amongst the buildings there is the oldest house still standing in Europe.

Orkney and the neighbouring islands of Shetland belonged to Norway until 1476. Kirkwall, the capital, was founded by Norsemen in the eleventh century. Its cathedral of St Magnus was founded in 1137.

Ring of Brogar, Orkney

St Magnus Bay, Shetland

Some ninety kilometres beyond Orkney lie the Shetland Isles. Here too there are fascinating connections with the past. The archaeological site of Jarlshof was lived in from the Bronze Age right through to Viking times. Shetland is nearer to Bergen than to Aberdeen, so Viking influence is strong. Each January, islanders celebrate the "Up Helly Aa" festival, when a replica Viking longship is burned to mark the end of winter.

Shetland has nearly five thousand kilometres of coastline with many natural harbours. One of these – Sullom Voe – has been developed as an oil terminal capable of taking the world's largest tankers.

Jarlshof

Mainland Scotland is divided in two by the Great Glen. This is more or less filled by three lochs linked by the ninety-six kilometre long Caledonian Canal, completed by Thomas Telford in 1822. Best known of the lochs is Loch Ness where the famous, but elusive, monster was first spotted by St Columba in the sixth century.

A famous early photograph of the Loch Ness Monster

Urquhart Castle and Loch Ness

Ben Nevis

Towering above Fort William at the western end of the
Caledonian Canal is Ben Nevis. At 1344 m, it is Britain's
highest mountain. To the south lies Glencoe, notorious
for the massacre of 1692 when thirty-eight Macdonalds
were murdered by visiting Campbells. Nowadays, the
Glen welcomes climbers and skiers.

First snow, Glencoe

Ullapool

Visitors to the Highlands may be surprised by the dozens of deserted villages they come across. These were abandoned during the Clearances of the late eighteenth and nineteenth centuries when people were driven from their homes to make way first of all for sheep and later, for large sporting estates. Many sought a new life overseas which accounts for the nineteen million Americans who are of Scottish descent!

Mainland Scotland's coastline is nearly four thousand kilometres long and inevitably fishing has always played an important part in the Scottish economy. Ullapool, in the far north-west, is one of Europe's busiest fishing ports. In recent years the local fishermen have been joined by huge East European factory ships known as "Klondykers".

It is only a short sea crossing to the Isle of Skye, famous in poetry and song. It is the largest of the Inner Hebrides and to many the most beautiful. The Gaelic description of Skye is "the isle of mist under the shadow of the great mountains." The jagged peaks of the Cuillins offer some of the most challenging climbing in the country. Skye is also famous for its connection with Bonnie Prince Charlie and Flora Macdonald, the girl who helped him to escape after the battle of Culloden.

Quirang, on the Isle of Skye

Loch Erisort, Isle of Lewis

Fishermen in Stornoway

Callanish Standing Stones

The Outer Hebrides form the western fringes of Britain, about twenty-five kilometres out from Skye. On this string of islands – Barra, Uist, Benbecula, Harris and Lewis – many families still work their small farms (crofts), cut peat for their fires, fish and weave. Handwoven Harris tweed is their most famous export, and it goes all over the world. There are over five thousand patterns of this traditional cloth.

Harris and Lewis in fact form one island, the largest in the Hebrides. Stornoway (this name means "anchor bay" in Norse) is the main town. There are many interesting archaeological sites amongst the bleak peat moors. They include the Callanish Standing Stones, second only to Stonehenge in size, and the broch at Dun Carloway. Brochs look very like power station cooling towers, but they are Iron Age forts, standing up to 12 m in height, found only in Scotland.

A forty-minute ferry trip from the busy port of Oban brings you to the Isle of Mull. Thirteenth-century Duart Castle, ancestral home of the Maclean clan, houses a museum of Scouting. Tobermory (which means

Mull

"the well of Mary" in Gaelic) is the largest village. The harbour, built by Thomas Telford, is a favourite berth for yachtsmen. Somewhere in Tobermory Bay lie the remains of a Spanish galleon which sank in 1588. The Mull Little Theatre in nearby Dervaig claims to be the world's smallest professional theatre.

Tobermory

Iona

Just off the west coast of Mull is the tiny island of Iona, sacred to the memory of St Columba who came here from Ireland with twelve fellow-missionaries in 563. In 802 Iona suffered the first of many attacks by Viking invaders. For centuries the island was the burial place of many kings: Scottish, Irish and almost certainly some French and Norwegian ones as well.

The thirteenth-century abbey has been beautifully restored by members of the present Iona Community, which consists of both church people and craftspeople.

Iona Abbey

Back on the mainland, New Lanark stands on the banks of the River Clyde, about two kilometres from the ancient burgh of Lanark. It is a remarkably preserved, planned village of the Industrial Revolution, associated

New Lanark

with the forward-looking mill owner of that time, Robert Owen. Unlike some mill owners, he improved working conditions and insisted that children went to his village school instead of the mill. Today, New Lanark is at the centre of a major conservation project.

The River Clyde is renowned for shipbuilding, and "Clyde built" has been the proud boast of many of the world's greatest liners. That included the *Queen Elizabeth*, launched in 1940 and still the largest ever to

Shipbuilding on the River Clyde

sail. Although there has been a decline in shipbuilding, the Clyde yards have responded by gaining orders from the Royal Navy and from the oil industry.

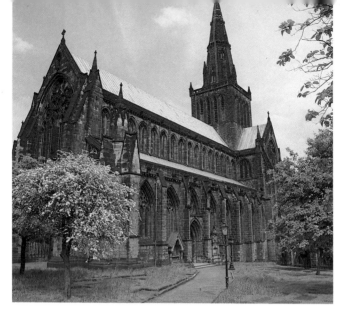

Glasgow Cathedral

Glasgow is generally thought of as a sprawling industrial city, a typical product of the Industrial Revolution. There is of course much more to Scotland's largest city. The Cathedral, founded by St Mungo (also known as St Kentigern), is the finest surviving example of the great religious buildings of pre-Reformation Scotland. The Lower Church dates back to the thirteenth century.

Provand's Lordship, built in 1471, is Glasgow's oldest house. Mary, Queen of Scots, is believed to have lived there while writing the famous "casket letters". It is now a museum.

Much of Glasgow of course does reflect the city's industrial past. The pride and ambition of Glasgow is typified in Templeton's Business Centre at Glasgow Green. Built in the 19th century as a carpet factory, it is a copy of the Doge's Palace in Venice. A reminder of the much humbler lives of the workers in such factories can be seen in the Tenement House, a typical Victorian tenement flat.

Inside Tenement House, Glasgow

George Square, Glasgow

George Square lies at the very heart of Glasgow. Like London's Trafalgar Square, it is usually thronged with visitors, or packed for parades and demonstrations. The most impressive building to be seen is the City Chambers, built in Italian Renaissance style and opened by Queen Victoria in 1888.

Glaswegians have a passion for football. There is always intense rivalry between Celtic and Rangers, the city's top clubs. Hampden Park is Scotland's national stadium.

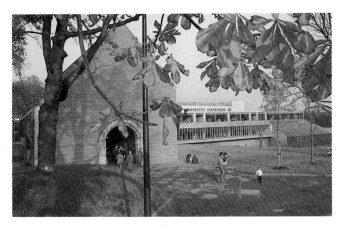

Standing in attractive Pollock Park is the award-winning building, opened in 1983, that houses the Burrell Collection. Given to the city by Sir William Burrell, a wealthy shipping magnate, the collection represents his love of beautiful objects. Of particular interest are the displays of ceramics, tapestries, furniture and pictures.

Culzean is one of Scotland's most popular tourist attractions. The Castle, designed by Robert Adam in 1777, overlooks a fine stretch of coastal scenery to the south of Ayr and is surrounded by an extensive country park. There is a walled garden dating from 1783, an aviary, a swan pond and a camellia house.

Scotland's national poet, Robert Burns, was born in Alloway in 1759. He put words to many of Scotland's most beautiful folk songs, and wrote such well-loved works as "Tam o'Shanter". Burns died in 1796. His birthday – 25th January – is celebrated world-wide, when traditionally, haggis is served with mashed potatoes and turnips. The dinner is followed by speeches and recitations in his honour, ending with the singing of "Auld Lang Syne". Burns' Cottage is now a museum and the start of the Burns' Heritage Trail.

Burns' Cottage, Alloway

Culzean Castle

Inside Burns' Cottage

49

Plockton, Highland

Glamis Castle, on Tayside

Although this has given you only a glimpse of Scotland,
perhaps it has shown you that it is indeed a land of
contrasts – mountain and sea, little fishing villages and
large, bustling cities, magnificent castles and crofters'

Mallaig

cottages. Scotland has a rich past and an exciting future. Above all, it is a land to stir the imagination with its beauty, history and romance.

River Affric, Highland

Index